SPIKE & IKE TAKE A HIKE

S. D. Schindler

NANCY PAULSEN BOOKS ✺ AN IMPRINT OF PENGUIN GROUP (USA) INC.

To STS, my hiking buddy.

NANCY PAULSEN BOOKS
A division of Penguin Young Readers Group.
Published by The Penguin Group.
Penguin Group (USA) Inc., 375 Hudson Street, New York, NY 10014, U.S.A.
Penguin Group (Canada), 90 Eglinton Avenue East, Suite 700, Toronto,
Ontario M4P 2Y3, Canada (a division of Pearson Penguin Canada Inc.).
Penguin Books Ltd, 80 Strand, London WC2R 0RL, England.
Penguin Ireland, 25 St. Stephen's Green, Dublin 2, Ireland (a division of Penguin Books Ltd).
Penguin Group (Australia), 250 Camberwell Road, Camberwell, Victoria 3124, Australia (a division of Pearson Australia Group Pty Ltd).
Penguin Books India Pvt Ltd, 11 Community Centre, Panchsheel Park, New Delhi - 110 017, India.
Penguin Group (NZ), 67 Apollo Drive, Rosedale, Auckland 0632, New Zealand (a division of Pearson New Zealand Ltd).
Penguin Books (South Africa) (Pty) Ltd, 24 Sturdee Avenue, Rosebank, Johannesburg 2196, South Africa.
Penguin Books Ltd, Registered Offices: 80 Strand, London WC2R 0RL, England.

Library of Congress Cataloging-in-Publication Data
Schindler, S. D.
Spike and Ike take a hike / S. D. Schindler.   p. cm.
Summary: "Spike the hedgehog and Ike the coatimundi go on a lively walk through the ever-changing landscape,
meeting other animals along the way"—Provided by publisher.
[1. Hedgehogs—Fiction. 2. Coatis—Fiction. 3. Animals—Fiction.] I. Title.   PZ7.S346352Spi 2013   [E]—dc23   2012010367
ISBN 978-0-399-24495-7
10 9 8 7 6 5 4 3 2 1

Lunch hunch . . .

Big bee

big bumblebee

big buzzy

bumblebee

big busy buzzy

bumblebee

Baby bird

blue-footed

baby bird

blue-footed booby baby bird

Soggy

bog

soggy

buggy bog

soggy froggy

buggy bog

Itty-bitty kitty

itty-bitty pretty kitty

itty-bitty pretty spitty kitty

Giraffe

giraffe

calf

giraffe calf

laugh

. . . Lunch

bunch

lunch bunch munch